MISSING!

Flame

Have you seen this kitten?

Flame is a magic kitten of royal blood, missing from his own world.
His uncle, Ebony, is very keen that he is found quickly.
Flame may be hard to spot as he often appears in a
variety of fluffy kitten colours but you can recognize him
by his big emerald eyes and whiskers that crackle with magic!

He is believed to be looking for a young friend to take care of him.

Could it be you?

If you find this very special kitten please let Ebony,
ruler of the Lion Throne, know.

Sue Bentley's books for children often include animals or fairies. She lives in Northampton and enjoys reading, going to the cinema, and sitting watching the frogs and newts in her garden pond. If she hadn't been a writer, she would probably have been a skydiver or a brain surgeon. The main reason she writes is that she can drink pots and pots of tea while she's typing. She has met and owned many cats and each one has brought a special sort of magic to her life.

Magic Kitten

Moonlight Mischief

SUE BENTLEY

Illustrated by Angela Swan

PUFFIN

To Misty, my grumpy blue-cream Persian girl

PUFFIN BOOKS

Published by the Penguin Group
Penguin Books Ltd, 80 Strand, London WC2R ORL, England
Penguin Group (USA) Inc., 375 Hudson Street, New York, New York 10014, USA
Penguin Group (Canada), 90 Eglinton Avenue East, Suite 700, Toronto, Ontario, Canada M4P 2Y3
(a division of Pearson Penguin Canada Inc.)
Penguin Ireland, 25 St Stephen's Green, Dublin 2, Ireland (a division of Penguin Books Ltd)
Penguin Group (Australia), 250 Camberwell Road, Camberwell, Victoria 3124, Australia
(a division of Pearson Australia Group Pty Ltd)
Penguin Books India Pvt Ltd, 11 Community Centre, Panchsheel Park, New Delhi – 110 017, India
Penguin Group (NZ), 67 Apollo Drive, Mairangi Bay, Auckland 1310, New Zealand
(a division of Pearson New Zealand Ltd)
Penguin Books (South Africa) (Pty) Ltd, 24 Sturdee Avenue, Rosebank, Johannesburg 2196, South Africa

Penguin Books Ltd, Registered Offices: 80 Strand, London WC2R ORL, England

penguin.com

Published 2006
2

Text copyright © Susan Bentley, 2006
Illustrations copyright © Angela Swan, 2006
All rights reserved

The moral right of the author and illustrator has been asserted

Set in Bembo
Typeset by Palimpsest Book Production Limited, Grangemouth, Stirlingshire
Made and printed in England by Clays Ltd, St Ives plc

British Library Cataloguing in Publication Data
A CIP catalogue record for this book is available from the British Library

ISBN-13: 978-0-141-32153-0
ISBN-10: 0-141-32153-9

Prologue

There was a flash of dazzling white light and silver sparkles. Where the young white lion had stood, now crouched a tiny kitten with long sandy fur. The sun beat down on a grove of nearby thorn trees.

An old grey lion ran up to the kitten and bowed his head. 'Prince Flame. You shouldn't be here. Your uncle Ebony searches for you,' Cirrus growled.

The kitten trembled but he stood up and shook himself. 'One day I will fight Ebony for the kingdom he has stolen from me!' he mewed bravely.

Cirrus nodded his shaggy head and his eyes glowed with affection. 'We all hope that day is soon, Prince Flame. But first you must grow strong and wise. Go far from here and hide in the other world once more, where you will be safe. Then return, to claim the Lion Throne.'

'Nowhere is safe from my uncle's spies . . .' Flame broke off as a deep terrifying roar rang out.

Cirrus moved quickly, shielding the tiny kitten with his body.

A huge black adult lion came from

behind a thorn tree. It lifted its head and sniffed the air. Suddenly it stiffened and its cruel eyes fastened on Cirrus.

'Ebony has your scent! Quickly, Flame! Go now!' Cirrus yowled urgently.

The adult lion snarled and bared its enormous teeth. It leapt forward and bounded towards Cirrus. Its mighty paws pounded the grass, and the ground beneath Flame's tiny paws shook.

Silver sparks glittered in Flame's long sandy fur and the kitten mewed as he felt the power building inside him. All sound faded. The ground seemed to sink beneath him and he felt himself falling. Falling . . .

Chapter
* ONE *

Eve Dawson stared gloomily out of the car as it came to a halt on the drive. There was a wooden sign by the front gate, which read, 'Ross Cattery. Open All Year.' A basket of cheerful purple and yellow pansies hung below the sign.

'Well, here we are. Right on time,' Mrs Dawson said brightly, glancing at her watch. 'Sally has arranged for someone to meet us here with a key.'

Maybe they'll have lost the key and we can go straight back home, Eve thought, getting out.

She stood with crossed arms, looking up at the grey stone house.

Mr Dawson came over and put his arm round Eve's shoulder. 'Cheer up, love. It's only for a few days, while Sally's away. You might even enjoy yourself.'

'Oh, right. Clearing up tons of smelly cat litter! My favourite way to spend half-term. Not!' Eve muttered.

She had reluctantly agreed to come and help her mum and dad look after the cattery only because she really liked the owner, Sally Ross. Sally was an old schoolfriend of her mum's. She never forgot Eve's birthday and always sent brilliant Christmas presents through the post. But Eve couldn't help thinking about her own schoolfriends who would be meeting up and having fun without her. She just wished the cattery was nearer home.

The door of a cottage across the road opened. A young woman, a girl and a little boy came out. The woman waved as they all crossed the road and came up the drive.

'Hello, everyone! I'm Jo Hinds. Sally's home help,' the woman said cheerfully. 'I've got a set of keys for you. I'll let you in and show you around. This is my daughter Alison and my son Darren.'

6

'Nice to meet you all,' Mr and Mrs
Dawson said.

Darren beamed up at Eve, his big
blue eyes sparkling. He had curly blond
hair and a sweet face and was clutching
a bright-red fire engine. Despite herself,
Eve smiled at the cute little boy who
looked about four years old.

Alison was tall with long brown hair
and looked about twelve. She had a

pretty face, which was spoiled by her sulky expression. She glanced at Eve. 'What's your name?' she asked abruptly.

'I'm Eve,' Eve said, smiling. 'It's nice to meet . . .' she began, but the older girl had already turned her back.

Alison stuck her hands in her jeans pocket and slouched after her mum who was showing Eve's parents through a side gate.

Eve stared after the older girl, surprised at her unfriendliness. But she shrugged and followed her. At the back of the house, a big L-shaped extension took up most of the garden. Near the house there was a tiny patio with a table and chairs. Tubs of plants stood in front of a fence. From the faint sounds

in the background, Eve guessed that
the cats' pens must be behind the
fence.

'I'll put the kettle on,' Jo said, once
they were all in the light, modern
kitchen. 'I've made some sandwiches.
Maybe we could all have lunch after
you've had a quick look round.'

Mrs Dawson smiled. 'Thanks, Jo.
That's very thoughtful of you.'

While her parents chatted to Jo, Eve wandered into the hall and then into the sitting room. It looked cosy, with red curtains and bookcases against one wall. There were two sofas and a bright rug in front of a huge stone fireplace. Polished horse brasses hung above the fireplace.

She heard someone come in behind her.

'It's not bad, is it? If you can stand looking at all those boring books.' Alison sauntered across the room. She threw herself on to one of the sofas and lay on her back, dangling her legs over one arm.

'Actually, I really like reading,' Eve said.

'It's OK, I suppose, if there's nothing else to do,' Alison said.

'Where are you, Alison? Wait for me!' called a voice.

Darren dashed into the room. He sprawled on the rug and ran his toy fire engine back and forth. 'Brr-rrrum! Brr-rrrm!' he said loudly.

Eve smiled. 'Darren seems really sweet.'

'Huh! You don't know him,' Alison muttered.

Just then Jo poked her head round the door. 'I'm going to take the Dawsons into the office and show them where things are. Why don't you take Eve up to see her bedroom, Alison? And could you keep an eye on Darren, please?'

'If I have to,' Alison said under her breath. As soon as her mum went out, she quickly swung her feet round and got up. She glanced at Darren who was completely engrossed in his game. 'Come on, quick! We'll leave him there,' she whispered to Eve.

'Are you sure . . . ?' Eve hesitated.

'Yes, I am! Hurry up!' Alison grabbed her arm and pulled her into the hall.

Eve couldn't help laughing as they raced up the stairs together. Alison darted into a bedroom, pulled Eve in behind her, and closed the door.

'That little pest won't find us in here,' she said, grinning.

Eve felt a bit mean for hiding from Darren, but she didn't want to say anything and risk upsetting Alison. She seemed to be trying to be friendly now. Eve looked round at her bedroom. The walls were yellow and the curtains and duvet were in cheerful stripes of yellow and white. The room seemed filled with sunshine. From the window, she could see over the patio fence to the rows of outdoor pens.

'This is a great room. You can see the yard and cat pens from up here,' Eve said excitedly.

'Glad you like it. Mum and I cleaned the house yesterday. I did all the hoovering by myself,' Alison said. 'Darren played with his toys, as usual. Mum never makes him do anything.'

Eve thought Darren looked a bit young to do chores, but she didn't say so. 'Does your mum come in every day?' she asked.

'Not usually, but she's going to while you're here.' Alison pulled a face. 'She's going to help with feeding the cats and stuff too. That's why I have to help her. It's a real pain. I'm never going to be able to see my friends.'

'I know what you mean,' Eve said with feeling. 'I keep thinking of all my friends back at home. Maybe *we* could go out for a pizza or rent a video sometime?'

Alison rolled her eyes. 'If I get desperate! I'm not that keen on hanging about with younger kids.'

'Please yourself!' Eve said, feeling her face grow hot. She hated the way she blushed when she was embarrassed or annoyed. It seemed like a waste of time trying to make friends with Alison. She quickly turned on her heel. 'I'm going to see what Mum and Dad are doing.'

Alison stood there, staring after her. 'Hey! I didn't mean . . .' she began.

'Forget it!' Eve called over her shoulder, already on her way downstairs.

In the kitchen, Eve saw that the door into the cattery office was open. She found her mum sitting at a computer, while Jo explained about the files and records. Her dad stood by, looking blank.

Mr Dawson winked at Eve as she came in. Eve pulled a sympathetic face. Her dad was useless with computers!

'Bedroom OK?' her dad asked. 'How are you getting on with Alison?'

'OK,' Eve said, still smarting a bit from the unfriendly comment. 'My bedroom's lovely. What's through here?'

'That's the storeroom. Go and have a look. It leads to the outdoor pens where the cats live.' He grinned. 'Meeting the cats is a certain cure for someone who had a long face all the way here!'

Eve put her hands on her hips.
'Da-ad! I'm not a baby any more! I'm
going to be eleven next birthday! And
I've got an even better cure. How
about letting me have my own pet
kitten?'

He chuckled, twinkling at her. 'Nice
try! What is this, pester power?' he
teased.

'If you like!' Eve laughed and gave her dad a playful shove. He could always cheer her up. And one day she *was* going to have a pet cat. She just needed to work on him a bit harder.

She went through the storeroom and straight outside to the rows of wire-mesh pens. They all had inside sleeping places and heat lamps for cold weather. In one pen, a Siamese cat was curled up in its bed. In another, Eve saw a tabby cat and a ginger kitten playing with a toy.

Suddenly, out of the corner of her eye, Eve saw a flash of bright white light. She spun round to see what seemed to be an empty pen glowing among all the others.

Eve frowned. What was that?

Curious, she went to have a closer
look.

'Oh!' she gasped.

There on the concrete floor crouched
a gorgeous, tiny kitten with long sandy
fur and the brightest emerald eyes Eve
had ever seen. Its fur and whiskers
seemed to be glowing with a thousand
tiny sparkles of light.

Eve blinked hard as she took a step
closer, but the sparkles seemed to have
died down and just the tiny sandy
kitten remained. Eve shook her head –
she must have been seeing things. She
was very tired from the long car
journey, after all.

She bent down to pat the kitten.
'Hello. Where did you come from?
And how did you get inside that pen?'

The kitten's little body trembled, but it sat up and looked straight at Eve with wide, scared, green eyes. 'I come from far away and my enemies are looking for me. Can you help me to hide, please?' it mewed.

Chapter
* TWO *

Eve stared at the kitten in utter amazement. Now she was hearing things as well as seeing things! She started to back off towards the house, but stopped. The tiny kitten looked so alone.

'You . . . you didn't really just speak to me, did you?' Eve stammered.

There was a pause and the sandy

kitten blinked slowly. 'Yes, I did. I am
Prince Flame.' Some of the fear seemed
to fade from his big emerald eyes.
'Who are you and what is your name?'

'I'm Eve. Eve Dawson. I'm . . . um . . .
looking after this cattery with my mum
and dad,' Eve answered hesitantly. Her
curiosity began to get the better of her
shock. 'Did you say *Prince* Flame?'

Flame nodded and lifted his tiny
sandy head proudly. 'I am heir to the
Lion Throne. My uncle Ebony has
stolen my throne and rules in my place.
His spies are searching for me. They
want to kill me.'

'Kill you?' Eve gasped. Flame was so
tiny and helpless-looking. She felt a burst
of protectiveness towards him. 'If any
nasty cats come here they'll have me to

deal with!' She had a sudden thought. 'Is your uncle a kitten like you?

'No. Ebony is enormous and very strong,' Flame growled softly, showing his little sharp teeth for the first time. 'But he and I are not cats.'

'Then what . . . ?'

There was a blinding silver flash. Eve couldn't see anything for a second and then her sight cleared. Where the cute kitten had been now stood a majestic young white lion.

Eve gasped and took a hasty step backwards.

Flame's fierce emerald eyes softened. 'Do not be afraid,' he said in a deep velvety roar. There was another flash and Flame was a cute sandy kitten with long silky fur once more.

'Well, I hope I never meet your uncle!' Eve said in a shaky voice. 'Come on, Flame. Let's hide. I'll take you into the house.'

As she bent down and picked Flame up, a few sparks from his fur tingled against her fingers before they went out. 'Just wait until I tell Mum and Dad all about you!'

'No! You must tell no one my secret.' Flame reached up and put a paw on her chest. He had a serious expression on his tiny face. 'Please promise, Eve.'

'All right. I promise. I'll just say you're a stray and I'm going to look after you,' Eve agreed disappointedly.

Her dad would have been as amazed and excited as she was about Flame, but a promise was a promise. She just hoped she could keep Flame's secret with so many people coming and going at the cattery.

Flame rubbed the top of his head against her arm and began purring loudly. 'That is good. Thank you, Eve.'

'I'm sorry, but keeping Flame is out of

the question,' Mrs Dawson said firmly. She had laid down the book she'd been reading. 'We've got more than fifty cats to look after, Eve. You can't really expect us to let you keep another one!'

Eve stared at her mum in utter dismay. 'But I *have* to look after Flame. He's in danger of . . .' She stopped in horror, realizing that she had been about to reveal Flame's secret. '. . . of starving or getting run over or even freezing to death!' she rushed on.

Her mum sighed. 'Don't be so dramatic, Eve! A stray could be carrying cat flu or anything. The responsible thing to do is contact the local pet centre.'

Eve felt tears of frustration pricking her eyes. She tried desperately to think of something to change her mum's mind. 'What about if we got Flame checked out by a vet? If he's given a clean bill of health, can I keep him?'

Mrs Dawson shook her head. 'I don't know . . .'

'Oh, please, Mum. You know I've

wanted a cat of my own for ages. If you let me keep Flame, I'll never pester you for anything ever again! He can sleep in my room and everything. You'll hardly even know he's here!'

Her dad came into the sitting room with a newspaper under his arm. 'What's all this? And where did that gorgeous little kitten come from? I haven't noticed him before.'

'I just found him . . .' Eve began.

Mary Dawson put a hand on her daughter's arm. She explained the situation, while her husband listened patiently. There was a pause when she'd finished speaking. Eve thought she might burst with the tension of waiting for her dad to speak.

'I suppose it wouldn't hurt to get the

little chap checked out, would it?' Jim Dawson said thoughtfully, at last.

'Yes!' Eve put Flame down on the sofa. She flew across the room and hugged her dad, silently promising herself to laugh at all his dreadful jokes for the next ten years. 'Mu–um?' Eve said in her best pleading voice, hoping desperately her mum would follow her dad.

Mary Dawson nodded. 'All right. We'll take Flame to the vet first thing tomorrow. But that doesn't mean you can keep him. We'll have another think about that later on.'

'OK, Mum,' Eve said meekly, picking Flame up again. She bent her head and whispered in his ear. 'Don't worry, she'll let you stay. I just know it.' Turning back to her parents, she said in a louder voice,

'I'm going to get some food for Flame and make him a bed in my room.'

Eve woke the following morning to the sound of loud purring in her ear.

She turned over and gave Flame a cuddle. His beautiful long sandy fur was the softest thing she had ever touched. 'Did you sleep well?' she asked him.

Flame's emerald eyes glowed with contentment. 'Very well, thank you. I feel safe here with you,' he mewed.

Eve tried not to think about the vet. What if he found that Flame had something wrong with him? Or even realized that Flame wasn't from this world? She felt her heart turn over at the thought of not being allowed to look after the gorgeous kitten.

Eve got up to feed Flame. She felt
too anxious to eat much breakfast
herself, but managed half a slice of
toast.

'Shut Flame in your bedroom for
now,' her mum said afterwards. 'I don't
want him near any of the cats until he's
been to the vet.'

Eve didn't argue. She didn't want to

do anything to make her mum change her mind. 'Sorry, Flame. It's only for a little while,' she said, stroking his little soft ears as she put him on the duvet.

Flame nodded. 'Very well. I will stay here.' He twitched his silky tail and settled down for a nap.

Eve helped her dad with the morning chores, while her mum dealt with a couple of new bookings. Jo, Alison and Darren arrived just as Eve was washing her hands at the sink in the storeroom. Alison came up to her.

'Hi, Eve,' Alison said brightly, coming straight over. 'Sorry I was in a bad mood yesterday. I . . .' she broke off as Eve looked past her.

Eve had spotted her dad coming

towards her with a pet carrier in one
hand and his car keys in the other. 'All
set, then? Go and fetch Flame, love.'

Alison frowned. 'Who's Flame?'

'My kitten!' Eve called as she dashed
up to her bedroom.

Alison stood looking after Eve with a
scowl on her face. 'You just can't
apologize to some people,' she
grumbled.

When Eve came back down with
Flame to put him inside the carrier,
Alison was nowhere in sight. 'Sorry, but
you have to travel inside this,' she
whispered to the tiny kitten as she
made him comfortable.

It was only a short journey to the
surgery, but Eve's stomach clenched
with nerves. When her name was

called, she took Flame into the treatment room and carefully lifted him on to the table.

'Hello there, little fellow,' the vet said in a friendly voice. 'What seems to be the trouble?' he asked Eve.

'I think he's fine. But Mum says Flame has to have a full health check,' Eve explained.

The vet smiled. 'Flame does look like a perfectly healthy kitten, but it's always best to make sure.' He checked Flame's fur for flea dirt, and then looked at his teeth, nose, eyes and under his tail. 'He's got a nice fat tummy, just like a kitten should have.'

Flame squirmed and miaowed indignantly at the vet's words.

Eve bit back a grin. She was sure that

Flame was dying to protest at being told he had a fat tummy and she wondered what the vet would say if he knew he was examining a royal magic kitten!

'Well, Flame's a picture of health,' the vet said finally.

On the way out, Flame licked his paw and washed his face. 'I could have told him that!' he purred to Eve, still looking quite put out.

Eve gave him a big cuddle.

Flame purred contentedly in the car on the way back as Eve stroked him through the mesh of the pet carrier.

'You're really taken with that kitten, aren't you?' her dad said.

'Yes, I am. I love him to bits, Dad,' Eve said. 'It already feels like Flame's lived with me for ever.'

'Oh, well. Now he's got a clean bill of health I think we might let him stay.'

Convincing her dad to let her keep Flame was only half the battle. Eve bit her lip. 'But . . . what about Mum?'

'You leave her to me,' her dad said with a wink.

Chapter
* THREE *

The following afternoon, Eve was
curled up with Flame on the sofa. A
big log fire burned in the grate. Leaves,
whipped up by the breeze, were
blowing past outside the window.

'I suppose I'd better go and give
Mum and Dad a hand,' she said,
reluctantly pushing herself to her feet.
'I'd much rather stay here with you,

Flame. But I'm on my best behaviour for the next couple of days. Just to be on the safe side with Mum.'

Flame stretched then yawned, showing his sharp little teeth. 'I will come with you.'

Eve heard Jo's angry voice floating out of the kitchen. She looked inside to see if her mum or dad were in there.

'What have I told you about keeping an eye on Darren, Alison? It's a good thing he only ate a few cat treats. Just imagine if he'd opened a tin of cat food!' Jo fumed.

Eve saw Alison leaning against the sink with folded arms, a sulky look on her face. 'That's it, blame me! Everything that goes wrong round here's always my fault!' she grumbled.

Darren sat at the kitchen table
drinking a glass of orange juice. He
shot Eve a cheeky grin, looking none
the worse for apparently having eaten
food meant for the cats.

Eve gave Alison a sympathetic smile,
before going off to find her parents.

Mr Dawson was in the storeroom.
He smiled when he saw Flame trotting

along behind Eve. 'I have to admit, Flame will be an unusually cute addition to the family. Just don't let him get under anyone's feet when we're busy, young lady.'

'I won't,' Eve promised, still feeling grateful to her dad. Whatever he had said to change her mum's mind about keeping Flame, it had worked like a dream. Flame was now an official member of the family!

Mr Dawson was loading a wheelbarrow with litter trays and clean cat litter. He wore a bright-red plastic apron, pink rubber gloves and blue wellies.

'What *do* you look like?' Eve said, holding both hands over her mouth to stop laughing.

'What?' Her dad looked down at himself. 'It's all the fashion on the Paris catwalks this year. Get it — catwalks?' he said, trying to keep a straight face.

Eve shook her head slowly as she got herself an apron and gloves. 'That's a terrible joke!'

She and Flame headed outside to the pens, while her dad trundled along behind them with the wheelbarrow. Even the boring task of changing litter trays was bearable with Flame for company.

Eve made friends with all kinds of cats. There were Siamese with slanting blue eyes, Persians with fluffy coats and flat faces, and all sizes and colours of ordinary household pets.

Flame nudged Eve's leg and looked

up at her with troubled eyes. 'What
have these cats done wrong, to be
punished by being kept in these cages?'
he mewed sadly.

Eve smiled gently as she bent down
to stroke him. 'They aren't being
punished. We're looking after them for
their owners while they're away. The
cats only stay here for a couple of
weeks and then they go back home.'

Flame looked very relieved. His tiny
face brightened when Eve stopped by a
pen with a big ginger and white cat
inside. The cat's name, Oscar, was on a
card attached to the mesh.

Eve bent down and pushed a finger
through the mesh. 'Hello, Oscar. You're
handsome, aren't you?' she said in a
gentle friendly voice.

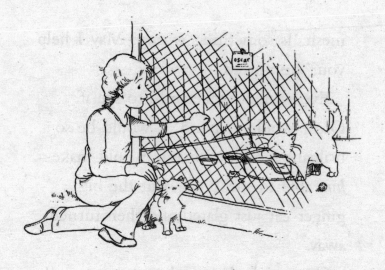

Oscar laid back his ears, bared his teeth and hissed loudly. He swung his thick tail back and forth.

'OK! I get the message!' Eve backed off with a smile. 'We'll come back and see him when he's in a better mood,' she said to Flame.

Flame gave a friendly little miaow and poked his nose through Oscar's mesh. 'Is something wrong? May I help you?' he purred.

Eve waited expectantly, to see if Oscar would respond. It would be so brilliant if Flame's magic would make *him* able to speak too. But the big ginger cat just glared and then turned away.

Flame sighed with disappointment. 'It seems my kind do not have the power to speak to cats in this world.' He glanced once more at Oscar, before following Eve to the next pen.

Eve had finished helping her dad and was washing her hands in the storeroom when her mum popped her head round the door. 'Eve!' she called. 'Would you mind nipping out for a jar of coffee? We've just run out.'

'No problem!' Eve jumped at
the chance of exploring the village
and shops. She grabbed her coat and
bag and was ready in two minutes
flat.

'Come on, Flame. Let's go,' she
said, slinging her bag over her shoulder
and holding the side gate open for
him.

Flame scampered ahead of Eve. His
sandy fur blew about in the wind as he
chased the leaves tumbling along the
path.

As they reached the supermarket, Eve
had a sudden thought. 'They don't
allow animals inside. You'd better get in
my bag.' She bent down so Flame
could jump in.

Once inside, she picked up a basket
and started looking for the coffee. She
wandered up and down, checking the
shelves and enjoying showing Flame
new things. As she drew near the toy
section, she heard a child shouting.

'No! I want one *now!*'

The voice sounded familiar. Eve
peeked round a corner and saw Darren

and Alison near a tall display of boxed toy cars. Darren was stamping his feet and yelling.

Alison had a shopping trolley loaded with groceries. Her back was turned to Eve. 'Stop acting like a two-year-old, Darren! You know you can't have one,' she said, wheeling her trolley around the end of the shelf. 'Come on. I'm going to pay for this lot now.'

'Don't care!' Darren yelled, staying behind in the empty aisle. He stretched forward and grabbed a box from near the bottom of the display.

Eve gasped as the huge pile of boxes shifted and the entire display slowly leaned towards Darren.

Time seemed to stand still. Eve felt a strange warm tingling up her spine. She looked down at her bag. Flame's head was sticking out. His silky fur was fizzing with a shower of silver sparkles and his whiskers crackled with electricity.

Eve tensed. It felt like something very strange was about to happen.

Chapter
* FOUR *

Lifting a tiny paw out of Eve's bag,
Flame sent a fountain of sparks towards
the collapsing display.

Suddenly there was a faint *pop!*
and Eve saw the heavy toy boxes
magically transform into a shower of
colourful glittering feathers, which
drifted down harmlessly around
Darren.

'Cool!' Darren clapped his hands. He kicked the feathers about and jumped up and down on them, completely forgetting about the toy cars. With sparkling feathers stuck all over him, Darren dashed after Alison, shouting, 'Come and look at this, Alison. Come and look!'

Eve gasped. What if anyone saw what

had just happened? Flame might be found out! She would have to warn him. 'Flame, you've got to . . .'

But before Eve could finish, Flame waved a sandy paw at the enormous pile of glittering feathers drifting across the shop floor. In another flash of silver sparks every single feather disappeared. The tall display of boxed cars stood neatly in their place.

Eve stared in amazement as the sparkles in Flame's silky fur gradually faded away. 'Phew! That was close. You were brilliant, Flame!'

'I am glad to help you, Eve,' Flame mewed, looking up at her with his big emerald eyes

Eve found the jar of coffee and went to pay for it. Alison and Darren were still at the checkout. Alison was packing groceries into plastic bags, while Darren looked out of the window.

'Shall I help you do that?' Eve said.

Alison glanced up. She looked all hot and fed up. 'You can if you want.'

Eve packed a bag and then carried it outside with Alison. Neither of them spoke. Darren took a ball out of his pocket and bounced it down the path.

'I heard Darren having a temper tantrum in the shop,' Eve said, to break the awkward silence.

Alison pulled a face. 'That's nothing new. He always plays up if he can't have something he wants.'

'What a pain!' Eve said sympathetically.

Alison nodded. 'I suppose he's no
worse than other kids. But he drives
me mad!' Her face suddenly broke into
a genuine smile. 'Thanks for helping
me with the shopping.'

'No problem,' Eve replied, returning
her smile.

Alison looked thoughtful. 'Mum said
I could go to the cinema tomorrow.
My friends are busy, so I was going by

myself. Do you want to come?'

'That would be great. I'll ask Mum and Dad if it's OK,' Eve said, really pleased that Alison had invited her. Maybe they could be friends after all, even after getting off to a bad start.

Suddenly Alison stiffened. 'Your shoulder bag! It just moved!'

Eve chuckled. 'Flame's inside. He comes everywhere with me, but I thought they wouldn't let me in the shop with him.' She opened her bag and lifted Flame out.

'Oh, isn't he swe-eet!' Alison crooned. She scratched Flame gently under the chin. 'Look at his gorgeous silky fur and green eyes! That's nice being able to bring your own cat with you from home.'

Eve was trying to decide how to
avoid complicated explanations, when
Darren came running up. He had
spotted Flame.

'I want to hold the kitten!' he
demanded.

Alison looked doubtful.

'It's OK, he can. Flame won't mind,'
Eve said, putting him into Darren's arms.

'Be very gentle and don't squeeze him,' Alison told her brother.

'Aw, he's cute! I want a kitten like this.' The little boy hunched over, cuddling Flame and gently stroking the top of his head. Flame wriggled about and whined softly.

Eve felt uneasy. What was wrong with Flame? He didn't seem to be feeling comfortable with Darren. As the little boy glanced up at Eve, she saw his blue eyes flash with mischief.

Alarm bells went off in her head. 'I'll have Flame back now, Da . . .'

But it was too late. Clutching Flame tightly to his chest, Darren pelted down the street and ran straight into a children's playground!

Chapter
* FIVE *

Eve shot after Darren. She ran into the
playground, which was crowded with
mums and children. She spotted Darren
at the back of a queue of little kids all
climbing a slide. Darren was two steps
from the top, when he slipped and
almost toppled backwards.

'Oo-er!' he cried, dropping Flame
and grabbing at the handrail.

'Miao-ow-ow!' Flame gave a howl of
fear as he managed to cling on to the
edge of the steps with his front paws.
His back legs scrabbled for a foothold,
but he was gradually slipping.

Eve realized that Flame couldn't use
magic in the crowded playground
without giving himself away. He was
going to fall at any moment.

She threw herself forward with her arms outstretched, just as Flame fell. She just managed to catch him before he crashed to the ground, but she fell on to one of her knees and winced as it twisted awkwardly.

'Oh, Flame. I was so scared you'd be killed,' Eve gulped, sprawled on the ground with the kitten in her arms.

Flame blinked up at her gratefully. 'Thank you for saving me, Eve,' he purred softly. 'But you have hurt yourself. Quickly, put me in your bag, so no one can see.'

Eve moved slightly and almost screamed as a sickening wave of pain shot up her leg. Biting her lip, she lifted Flame back into her bag, just as a burst of silver sparks crackled in his fur.

There was a warm, tingling sensation in her knee and she felt the pain draining away, just as if she had poured it down a sink.

Seconds later, Flame emerged from the bag.

'Thanks, Flame. My knee feels good as new,' Eve whispered. She got up with Flame still in her arms and looked round for Darren.

She saw Alison, who had just run into the playground with all the shopping and had grabbed Darren as he shot off the end of the slide. She was as white as a sheet as she hugged her little brother tightly. 'Don't you ever run off like that again! I thought you were going to fall right down those stairs!' she said shakily.

Eve went over to Alison. 'Is Darren all right?'

Alison nodded. 'He's fine. How's Flame?'

'He's all right now,' Eve said. She looked at Darren. 'It was very naughty to run off with Flame like that. You could have hurt him badly.'

Darren sniffled and rubbed his eyes. 'It wasn't me!' he said defiantly.

'I'm really sorry. You can see what he's like, can't you?' Alison looked hopefully at Eve. 'You won't say anything to Mum about him running off, will you?'

Eve considered for a moment. Darren definitely wasn't the little angel he first seemed! But it wasn't Alison's fault he'd run off. 'No, I won't say anything,' she decided. 'But maybe you should tell your mum how Darren plays you up.'

Alison smiled gratefully. 'I'll think about it. Thanks, Eve. You're OK.'

'Can I go to the cinema with Alison tomorrow, Dad?' Eve asked early that evening as she helped make a salad to go with the lasagne her dad was making. Her mum was busy in the office, booking in a new cat, so her dad had offered to cook supper.

'That sounds like a good idea. You must have been missing going out with your friends back home,' Mr Dawson said, ruffling her blonde hair.

'I was a bit at first, when I didn't really know Alison,' Eve admitted. 'But I do have the best friend anyone could wish for — Flame!'

Flame looked up from his dish of tuna flakes and gave an extra-loud purr.

Her dad chuckled. 'I think Flame agrees! And I'm glad you and Alison are getting on now.' He paused. 'On another subject altogether, that grumpy ginger and white cat didn't eat much food again. I hope he isn't getting sick.'

'Oscar?' Eve guessed.

'He's one of your favourites, isn't he? I think we'll get him checked over by the vet.' Her dad popped the supper in the oven. 'I'm just going to the office. I'll get your mum to phone Oscar's owners when she has a minute, to tell them what's happening.'

Curious, Eve decided she'd go and

have a quick look at Oscar herself.

'Come on, Flame,' she called, as the little kitten padded along behind her.

As soon as she opened Oscar's pen and stepped inside with Flame, the grumpy cat pricked up his ears. Oscar gave a low growl in his throat and then he spotted Flame. His eyes narrowed with interest as he walked over to the kitten and had a good sniff. A moment later, Oscar started purring.

'He seems to like you, Flame,' Eve said in amazement. 'I wonder if Dad's right about Oscar being sick.' She risked stroking Oscar gently. He put up with it for a second or two and then moved away. 'Poor old boy. Do you feel poorly? Is that why you're grumpy?' *It's a shame you can't talk, like Flame,* she thought. *Then you could tell us what's wrong.*

Chapter
★ SIX ★

'Hurrah, it's Saturday! My favourite day!' Eve cried the following morning as she dried her hair after having a shower.

Flame sat on the bedroom window sill, washing his face with the side of one front paw. He gave her a whiskery grin. 'Why do you like this day so much?'

'Because it's when I get my pocket money!' Eve said in a voice muffled by the towel over her head. 'And I'm going to the cinema!'

Flame frowned. 'What is the cinema? It sounds as if it is a good place.'

'Oh, it is. It's where they show moving pictures, called films. They can be funny or sad or even frightening. You can buy popcorn to eat too. It's great fun.'

Flame's eyes widened. 'I would like to see these moving pictures. Will you take me with you?' he purred excitedly.

'Of course I will,' Eve promised. 'But you'll have to hide in my bag again.'

Flame nodded. 'And what is this popcorn you eat? Is it something like cat biscuits?'

Eve bit back a grin. 'Not exactly. I think you'll want to pass on the popcorn!'

She finished drying her hair and then reached for her shoulder bag. Flame jumped inside and curled up.

As she went to call for Alison, Eve couldn't help thinking about Oscar. The vet had kept him at the surgery as he wanted to do some tests.

Alison opened her front door, wearing just a long baggy T-shirt and slippers.

Eve thought she must have forgotten about going to the cinema. 'Hi, Alison! You'd better hurry or we'll miss the start of the film,' she said.

'I'm . . . I'm not coming,' Alison gulped. Her eyes looked red and puffy as if she'd been crying. 'Darren's been playing up again. Mum's gone ballistic and now I'm grounded.'

'What's he been up to?' Eve asked.

Alison wiped her eyes. 'I was doing my homework in the kitchen, when Darren sneaked upstairs. He got hold of Mum's lipsticks and rubbed them all over the duvets and bedroom curtains. It took Mum hours to get the stains out.'

'But that wasn't your fault,' Eve said indignantly.

Alison shrugged. 'Try telling my mum that. I explained that Darren slipped past without me noticing, but she said I should have checked on him. The little horror was quiet as a mouse up there. You know what he's like.'

'Yes, I do,' Eve said with feeling, remembering how Darren had run off with Flame. 'I'm really sorry you can't come out today. Maybe we can go to the cinema another time.'

Alison nodded and gave her a watery smile. 'Yeah, OK,' she murmured, before shutting the door.

'Poor Alison. She was really upset,' Eve said to Flame as they retraced their steps back to the cattery. 'I don't know how she puts up with that little terror of a brother!'

'Whose daft idea was it to volunteer to look after the cattery?' Jim Dawson groaned on Sunday afternoon as he stretched and yawned.

Eve giggled and gave him a playful shove. 'Mum's and yours, silly!'

Her dad chuckled. 'Well, next time I

have an idea like that, someone shoot me!'

Eve made everyone some hot chocolate. She took a mug in to her dad and then went into the office where her mum was catching up with some paperwork.

'Thanks, love.' Mary Dawson took the hot chocolate and sipped gratefully. 'I've almost finished here. I thought we could all go out for a brisk walk and blow the cobwebs away.'

Eve put her head on one side. 'Do you mind if I don't come, Mum? I was planning to watch that new video Dad got for me, seeing as how I didn't get to go to the cinema with Alison.' Eve was looking forward to showing Flame what video and TV was like!

Her mum patted her arm. 'No, that's
fine, love. How about you, Jo? Do you
and Darren fancy coming?'

Jo had just popped in to deliver a
pile of ironing. Darren was outside the
back door, kicking a ball against the
terrace wall. Jo smiled. 'A walk's
probably just what Darren and I need.
And it'll give Alison a bit of peace

while she's doing her homework.'

Eve felt pleased that Alison had some peace and quiet for a change, especially after the lipstick disaster. Even though she sometimes felt a little lonely without any brothers or sisters, she didn't envy her having a brother like Darren.

After everyone had gone out, Eve decided she needed some crisps and a drink to go with the video. She looked in the kitchen cupboard, but they were out of crisps. Now that she'd set her heart on them, nothing else would do.

'Come on, Flame. We'll just have to go and buy some treats,' she said, pulling on a jacket.

It was windy in the street. Yellow and green leaves scuttled along in little whirlwinds along the pavement. Flame couldn't resist them. He darted about play-growling and pouncing on leaves, his sandy tail whisking about with excitement.

At the shop Eve bought some crisps and chocolate and a big bottle of lemonade. As she came back, she passed Alison's house. On impulse, she decided to ask Alison if she'd like to come and watch the video too.

'I bet she'll be glad to get away from doing boring homework,' she said to Flame, as she knocked on the front door.

Alison took ages to answer. Eve was about to give up, when the door opened a crack.

'Hi,' Eve said brightly. 'Dad rented a

video for me. Do you fancy coming to watch it with Flame and me?'

'Oh, er . . . Hi, Eve,' Alison puffed, out of breath.

Her cheeks were pink and her long brown hair was all over the place. Eve noticed there was a sticking plaster on the older girl's finger. It looked new, as if Alison had just put it on. 'Have you cut your finger?' Eve asked worriedly.

'No! I mean . . . I . . . er . . . burned it on the toaster. Silly, isn't it?' She gave Eve an awkward grin. 'A video sounds great. Thanks. I'll just grab my coat.'

Eve raised her eyebrows at Flame. Alison was acting really oddly.

Alison reappeared in her coat.

'Ready? Let's go.'

Back at the cattery, Eve, Alison and

Flame settled down in the sitting room. The video was fun. It was a brilliant fantasy adventure. Flame curled up on Eve's lap, watching it intently and purring loudly.

Alison grinned. 'Fancy that kitten liking films. It's amazing.'

Eve just smiled, thinking that Flame was even more amazing than Alison realized!

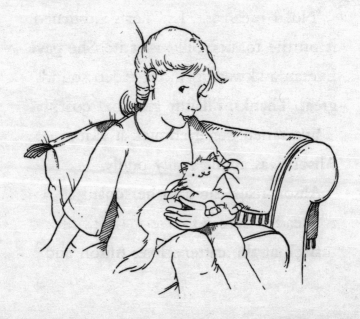

As Eve took the video out of the player, her parents, Jo and Darren came in. They were all flushed and wind-blown from their walk.

'Can I play in the garden?' Darren asked.

'I wish I had that boy's energy,' Mrs Dawson said with a smile, going into the kitchen after Darren. 'I'll make us all a hot drink.'

'Hello, what are you doing here, Alison? I thought you were doing your homework,' asked Jo, frowning.

'That was my fault,' Eve said quickly. 'I asked her over to watch a video. That's OK, isn't it?'

Jo's face softened as she smiled at Alison and Eve. 'Course it is. It's nice that you two are spending time

together. You can always finish your
homework later, Alison.'

Alison rolled her eyes at Eve.
'Thanks,' she whispered. 'I thought I
was in trouble for a minute there!'

Eve chatted to her dad, Jo and Alison
for a couple of minutes and then
decided to go and see if her mum
wanted any help. Flame followed her
into the kitchen.

'What's that noise, Mum?' Eve said, as
she heard some scuffling and clanging
coming from outside. She looked out
of the kitchen window, expecting to
see Darren kicking his ball around, but
he wasn't on the patio. 'It's coming
from over the fence. Something's going
on near the pens. Come on, Flame.
Let's go and have a look.'

Her mum frowned. 'Wait a minute, love. I'll get your dad.'

But Eve and Flame were already rushing through the storeroom and running out into the yard. Eve stopped, her eyes widening with dismay as she saw the terrible mess.

The rubbish bins had been tipped over. Newspapers, food packaging and empty tins had spilled everywhere. And right in the middle of the rubbish, kicking tins and packets about, was Darren.

Chapter
* SEVEN *

Eve's parents and Jo came out into the yard. 'Oh, no!' Mr and Mrs Dawson gasped.

Jo ran over to Darren. 'You naughty boy! Whatever possessed you to do this?' she shouted.

Darren looked up at his mum with innocent blue eyes. 'It wasn't me!'

Jo bent down in front of her son.

'You're only making it worse by telling fibs!'

'I'm not!' Darren insisted, sticking out his bottom lip. 'It wasn't me.'

Jo looked really embarrassed as she turned towards the Dawsons. 'I'm really sorry about this! I'll take Darren home and then come back and help clear up this mess. Alison, will you stay at home with him, please?' she called to her daughter who stood in the doorway.

Alison's shoulders slumped and she sighed heavily. 'Why me?' she complained. Then she saw her mum's expression. 'OK, if I have to,' she said in a small voice.

Darren's angelic face crumpled. He howled in protest as his mum marched him away.

Mrs Dawson sighed. 'Jo seems very
upset. I think I'll go inside and have a
word with her.'

'All right,' her husband said as he
began gathering up sheets of
newspapers. Eve picked up some
packets and reached for a couple of
tins. 'Careful you don't cut yourself,
love. Those are sharp,' her dad warned.
'You'd best put some thick gloves on.

Oh, that's the phone now. I'll be right back.'

'Darren is such a pest!' Eve said to Flame. She reckoned you needed three eyes to watch him. Two in the front and one in the back of your head. 'This mess is going to take ages to clear up.'

Flame gave a short miaow. 'Do not worry, Eve. I will help you.'

Eve felt the familiar tingle up her spine as Flame's sandy fur ignited with silver sparks and his whiskers crackled and fizzed. Eve couldn't wait to see what would happen next! Flame pointed a tiny paw, his emerald eyes flashing with concentration. Suddenly a comet's tail of glittery light shot all round the rubbish-strewn paved area.

Bang! The bins stood to attention and

opened their lids. Rustle! Newspapers rose up high into the sky and then fluttered back down into the bottom of the bins. Crunch and clunk! The packets, boxes and tins marched one behind the other, like toy soldiers, right up to the bins and then shot inside.

Eve clapped her hands in delight as the bins snapped shut – not a single piece of the mess Darren had made remained. 'Thanks, Flame. That was fantastic!'

'You are welcome.' Flame sneezed as a final spark tickled his nose and then faded before Eve's eyes.

A few minutes later, Eve's dad came back out into the yard. 'Another owner wanting to book their cat in . . .' He broke off in amazement as he noticed that every bit of rubbish was all gone.

'Goodness me! However did you manage to clear up so quickly?'

Eve gave him a broad grin. 'Oh, I'm full of magic tricks!' *At least, Flame is,* she thought, wishing she could tell everyone how special Flame really was.

'That was the vet. He wants to have a chat about Oscar,' Mary Dawson said the following afternoon, replacing the phone. 'I'm going to pop over there now.'

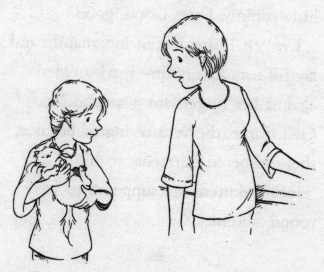

'Can Flame and I come with you?'
Eve asked eagerly.

'All right,' her mum agreed.

'I'll meet you at the car!' Eve jumped
up and went to fetch a pet carrier for
Flame.

At the surgery, the receptionist took
them straight through to a treatment
room. Eve was carrying Flame in her
arms. 'Hello again,' the vet said, when
he saw Eve and Flame. 'Still got his fat
little tummy, I see. Good, good.'

Eve felt Flame stiffen indignantly and
lay his ears flat. A tiny spark tingled
against her fingers for a second. 'It's
OK, Flame, the vet's trying to be nice,'
she whispered hurriedly to him.
'Healthy kittens are supposed to have
round tummies.'

Flame relaxed and pricked up his ears.

The door opened and a nurse brought Oscar in and put him on the table. Eve put Flame down on the table beside Oscar. Flame mewed softly and rubbed his sandy head against the older cat's leg. Oscar touched noses with the kitten and began purring softly.

'Hello, boy. How are you?' Eve stroked Oscar as she listened to the vet. He explained that Oscar had something with a very long, complicated name, which some cats developed as they grew older.

'But is he going to get better?' Eve asked worriedly.

The vet nodded. 'Oh, yes. He's had some medicine and he's already feeling much better. Once he gets his appetite back, he'll be just like his old self.'

'That's brilliant!' Eve exclaimed. She felt so pleased that Oscar was going to be OK. Flame seemed delighted too and even seemed to have forgotten to be cross with the vet!

Back at the cattery Eve and Flame took Oscar to his pen and made him comfortable. She discovered some of her dad's favourite prawns in the kitchen fridge and pinched a couple as a treat for Oscar. 'Here you are, Flame. There's a few for you too. Dad won't miss them!'

Flame chomped down the prawns and then licked his lips to get every last fishy taste. 'That was delicious. I like this human food!'

The rest of the afternoon passed quickly. Eve helped her dad for a while and then gave Jo a hand cleaning pens with disinfectant. When a delivery of dried cat food arrived from a pet-food supplier, she showed the driver where to put the sacks.

Darren was on his best behaviour. He stayed by Alison's side while Jo worked, and even made a big fuss of Flame. Eve thought he seemed sorry for running off with Flame the other day.

She felt really tired by the time she went upstairs and crawled into bed. Rain pattered against the bedroom window. She drifted slowly off to asleep to the sound of it, with Flame's warm furry little body curled up next to her.

Eve woke up with a start.

She sat up, blinking in the darkness, trying to work out what it was that had woken her. She listened carefully. Every now and then, she was sure she could hear faint sounds coming from outside.

'Can you hear that?' she whispered to Flame.

'Yes, I can. Someone is out there,' the

little kitten mewed softly, jumping across to the window sill.

Eve's heart beat fast. She got out of bed and peeped out of the curtain. It was still raining. The terrace with its table and chairs looked shiny in the darkness. Beyond the terrace wall, the extension and the cat pens looked dim and shadowed.

As the moon slipped out from behind a cloud, Eve froze. The storeroom door leading to the yard was wide open. She watched as a slim dark figure came out dragging something that looked heavy. It was only then that she noticed the dark humps already lying out on the paved area.

A burglar was stealing the sacks of cat food!

'Come on, Flame, we have to stop them!' Eve said, already dashing for the door and racing downstairs in her pyjamas.

With Flame streaking ahead of her, Eve rushed into the extension. A blast of cold air met her as she ran outside. She could see the dark figure a short distance away in the yard, bending over a sack of food. It was wearing dark trousers and a top with the hood up.

'Stop, thief!' Eve meant to shout, but it came out as a dry croak. She tried again, this time yelling at the top of her voice. 'STOP, THIEF!!'

'Wha . . . !' The figure almost jumped out of its skin with shock. It straightened up and started hurrying towards the gate at the side of the cottage.

Eve didn't think twice. She ran after the burglar, but Flame was even faster. He hurtled towards the gate and scrabbled up it until he stood balanced on the top. His sandy fur bristled as he arched his tiny back. Hissing fiercely, he faced the burglar.

Eve's heart hammered in her chest. Flame was so brave. She could imagine just what he would be like as a Lion

Prince, even though here he couldn't use any magic or he'd give himself away. Eve felt sick with fear for him.

The hooded figure raced up to the gate and grabbed the catch. 'Get off! Go away!' the burglar shouted at Flame.

Eve's eyes widened in shock. It was a girl's voice! One she recognized.

Flame recognized the burglar too. He gave a loud whine and jumped into the girl's arms. The burglar took a step backwards, holding Flame. She turned round slowly to face Eve as Eve pushed back her hood.

'Alison!'

Chapter
* EIGHT *

Eve sat with Flame huddled inside her dad's fleece jacket. Her bare feet stuck out of her rain-soaked pyjama bottoms. From the look in her dad's eyes, she knew she was in for an awesome telling-off for running outside in the middle of the night by herself.

At least the cat food hadn't got too wet. It was all back inside the storeroom and her mum had assured everyone that it would be fine.

Alison sat opposite Eve, looking shamefaced. Mr and Mrs Dawson sat on either side of her.

'But why, Alison?' Mrs Dawson asked gently. 'What did you hope to gain by stealing the cat food?'

'I wasn't stealing it. I just wanted it to get wet, so everyone would be furious with Darren. You were supposed to think he'd dragged the food out,' Alison said miserably.

Eve's dad looked at his wife. 'Am I missing something?'

Eve thought she was beginning to work it out. 'You wanted everyone to see what hard work Darren really was?' she said to Alison, remembering the supermarket.

Alison nodded. 'I wanted Mum to
see, so that she would have to look
after Darren and it wouldn't be just up
to me to watch him all the time. But
she wouldn't listen.'

Flame gave a little mew of sympathy
and brushed against Alison's ankle. She
leaned down to stroke him.

Mr and Mrs Dawson looked at each
other in amazement.

Something else fell into place for

Eve. She remembered the day when she'd called round to Alison's house with the video. Alison had been really out of breath when she'd answered the door. Then there was the new plaster on her finger.

'You didn't burn your finger, did you? You cut it when you tipped all the rubbish out!' Eve burst out. 'No wonder you were puffed out. You'd only just rushed back home, when I knocked on your front door!'

Alison hung her head, nodding. 'Eve's right. I tipped out the rubbish, so that Darren would get the blame. I know I've been really stupid. Are . . . are you going to call the police?'

Her mum and dad looked at each other.

Eve stared at her parents in horror.
'You aren't going to, are you? They'll
probably handcuff Alison and throw her
into a cell. And she'll only get bread
and water to eat . . .'

'That's enough, Eve,' her dad said
with a faint smile. 'I think it's time we
took Alison home and I had a word
with her mum.' He gave Eve a firm,
direct look. 'And as for you, young
lady, you can go straight back to bed.'

Eve knew when her dad meant business. She rose to her feet and then picked Flame up. 'OK,' she said in a subdued voice.

Alison looked back from the doorway, her eyes bright with tears. 'I'm really sorry for what I've done. Will you still be friends with me, Eve?'

Eve only hesitated for a second. 'Of course I will. And Flame will too.'

'Jo was pretty surprised and upset when she heard about what Alison had been up to,' Mrs Dawson told Eve the following morning. 'But Alison seems genuinely sorry. She's even offered to buy Darren the toy car he wants with her pocket money. I persuaded Jo that no real harm's done. She's decided to make sure

Alison has more time for herself, without Darren tagging along too. I expect the whole thing will soon blow over.'

'That's brilliant! Well done, Mum,' Eve said warmly. Her mum was really good at calming people down.

'But as for you, young lady . . .' her dad said.

'I know!' Eve said quickly.

She still felt really guilty for worrying her parents. Her dad said he couldn't believe his eyes when he'd seen her in her pyjamas, chasing what appeared to be a burglar!

'I've already promised Mum that I won't ever, ever, ever do anything like it again,' she said now, making cross-my-heart movements with one finger. 'And I really mean it.'

'I'm sure you do. Until next time?'
her dad said with a twinkle in his eye.
'Let's forget all about it. Where's Flame
this morning? He usually follows you
everywhere.'

'I know.' Eve felt an odd little pang.
Flame had been strangely reluctant to
come downstairs with her. She had left
him curled up on her duvet.

'I'll go and fetch him now,' she said,
making for the stairs.

'Flame?' Eve called, as she went into her bedroom. But there was no sign of him. She looked behind the curtain and under the bed. 'Where are you?' she said, starting to feel anxious.

There was a faint whimper from beneath a chest of drawers. Eve bent down. She saw Flame crouched right at the back against the wall.

'What's wrong, Flame?'

'My enemies are getting near. I can sense them,' he yowled worriedly. He crawled out slowly, keeping his tummy low to the ground. His big green eyes were huge and scared.

Eve picked him up. As she stroked Flame's long sandy fur, she felt his tiny body trembling. 'It's OK. You're safe with me. You . . . you don't have to leave, do you?' she asked hesitantly. 'I'll look after you, I promise.'

She had been looking forward so much to taking Flame home with her.

Flame shook his head. 'Not yet. But if my uncle's spies come any closer, then I must leave at once.'

Eve held him close. She rubbed her chin gently on the top of his little head. 'I don't want you to go. I want you to stay with me for ever,' she whispered, refusing to think of losing her special friend.

Flame purred softly, but his emerald eyes remained troubled.

C h a p t e r
* NINE *

'It's our last day at the cattery.
Sally will be back tonight. And we're
all going home early tomorrow.
Including you!' Eve told Flame
excitedly.

Flame seemed more relaxed and the
fearful look had faded from his eyes.
Eve hoped like mad that Flame's
enemies were hundreds of miles away.

It was too painful to think of going home without him.

'Shall we go and see Oscar?' she suggested, deciding to change the subject.

Flame gave an eager little mew. 'Yes, I would like that.' He ran along beside Eve, his silky tail sticking up jauntily.

Oscar was sitting having a wash. As soon as he saw Eve and Flame he came trotting over. Eve let herself into the pen and crouched down to stroke the big ginger and white cat. Flame purred and licked Oscar's ears. Eve smiled as Oscar rubbed his head against the tiny kitten.

'Are we friends now then, Oscar?' Eve said. 'You're not really grumpy, are you, boy? You were just sick and a bit lonely.'

After she closed Oscar's pen, she went to find her mum and report on his progress.

Mrs Dawson was on the office phone. 'That's such a shame. But I understand. Poor Oscar. I've got a couple of numbers I can ring. I'll let you know how I get on. Goodbye.'

'What's wrong?' Eve asked.

Her mum frowned. 'Oscar's owners were very upset. They've just found out they have to move house because of their work. There's a strict rule that no pets are allowed, so it looks like Oscar might have to be rehomed.'

'Oh, no,' Eve said, feeling upset. It didn't seem fair after all poor Oscar had been through.

She tried not to think about Oscar as she helped with the usual chores, but she couldn't seem to get him out of her mind.

Jo, Darren and Alison had come in early. With Sally coming back, everyone was working extra hard to have the cattery looking its best.

Alison had a quiet word with Eve.

'Mum's been great about everything. She says I won't need to help out with Darren as much when Sally's back. And Darren's going to be starting nursery school in a few weeks, so he'll be happier too.' She grinned. 'He'll have lots more kids to run around and be mischievous with!'

As Eve helped with a few last chores, she felt a bit sad. She was going to miss looking after all the cats, especially Oscar. Then she brightened up; having Flame with her was going to be fantastic. She couldn't wait to show him to all her friends.

Her dad came in as Eve was stacking clean food dishes into a cupboard. 'In a few hours, we'll be on our way. Who would have thought that we'd be taking *two* cats home with us?'

Eve stared blankly at him. 'Two cats? Flame and . . . ?' Suddenly the penny dropped. 'Oscar!'

'Yes, Oscar!' her dad said, laughing at the delighted expression on her face. 'We're adopting him. Your mum and I can see that you've grown really fond of him.'

Eve felt a warm glow in her chest. 'Do you really mean it?' She flung her arms round her dad. 'That's wonderful!'

She rushed off to tell Flame the good news. He was going to be so pleased. She had left him sniffing about in the yard in front of the cat pens.

Flame looked up and mewed a greeting as she came towards him.

Suddenly Eve glimpsed fierce, shadowy cat shapes behind Flame. They were peering into the pens. Her heart missed a beat.

'Flame, look out!' she cried.

Acting on instinct, she grabbed the water hose used to flush out the pens. Turning it on, she aimed a jet of water at Flame's enemies. The cat shapes slunk back, trying to avoid a soaking.

There was a flash of dazzling bright
light. Flame was no longer a tiny sandy
kitten but instead stood in front of Eve
as a magnificent young white lion once
more. At his side this time was an
older, adult grey lion.

Flame lifted his regal head and
looked at Eve with sad green eyes. 'Be
well, Eve,' he growled in a deep velvety
voice. He raised a large white paw in
farewell and then was gone.

There was a terrifying howl of rage from the fierce dark cats, before they too disappeared.

Eve stood alone in the yard. A deep sadness welled up in her. She couldn't believe Flame had had to go so suddenly. She was relieved that Flame was safe, but she was going to miss him terribly.

'I'll never forget you, Flame,' she whispered as her eyes pricked with tears. She knew that she would always treasure the time she had shared with the tiny magic kitten.

Wiping her eyes, she turned on her heel and went towards Oscar's pen as she thought about how to tell her mum and dad. Somehow she knew that Flame was watching with a smile of approval in his big emerald eyes.

Win a Magic Kitten goody bag!

An urgent and secret message has been left for Flame
from his own world, where his evil uncle is
still hunting for him.

Two words from the message can be found in royal lion
crowns hidden in *Moonlight Mischief* and *A Circus Wish*.
Find the hidden words and put them together to complete
the message. Send it in to us and each month we will
put every correct message in a draw and pick out one lucky
winner who will receive a purrfect Magic Kitten gift!

Send your secret message, name and address on a postcard to:
Magic Kitten Competition
Puffin Books
80 Strand
London WC2R 0RL

Hurry, Flame needs your help!

Good luck!

puffin.co.uk

Visit:
penguin.co.uk/static/cs/uk/0/competition/terms.html
for full terms and conditions

A Circus Wish

Flame needs to find a purrfect new friend!

And that's how Sadie's
circus adventure begins
when adorable coal-black
kitten Flame tumbles
into her life . . .

Magic Kitten

Classroom Chaos
0–141–32015–X

A Summer Spell
0–141–32014–1

Star Dreams
0–141–32016–8

Moonlight Mischief
0–141–32153–9

Double Trouble
0–141–32017–6

A Circus Wish
0–141–32154–7

Coming Soon . . .

Sparkling Steps
0–141–32155–5

A Glittering Gallop
0–141–32156–3

puffin.co.uk